P9-CDO-889

3 4028 10223 0324
HARRIS COUNTY PUBLIC LIBRARY

J Marsh
Marsh, Carole
The mystery at Mount Fuji :
Tokyo, Japan

FEB 14 2020

$7.99
ocn164217681

Wh...
Carole...

I love the real locatio...
want to go and visit t...
My Mom says maybe, but I can't wait!

One day, I want to be a real kid in one of Ms. Marsh's

Presented to

Spring Branch Memorial Library

By

**Friends of Spring Branch
Memorial Library**

: Harris County
Public Library

your pathway to knowledge

made up. Trying to figure that out is fun!

Grant is cool and funny! He makes me laugh a lot!!

*I like that there are boys and girls in the story of different
ages. Some mysteries I outgrow, but I can always find a
favorite character to identify with in these books.*

*They are scary, but not too scary. They are funny. I learn a
lot. There is always food which makes me hungry. I feel like
I am there.*

What Parents and Teachers Say About Carole Marsh Mysteries . . .

I think kids love these books because they have such a wealth of detail. I know I learn a lot reading them! It's an engaging way to look at the history of any place or event. I always say I'm only going to read one chapter to the kids, but that never happens—it's always two or three, at least!
—Librarian

Reading the mystery and going on the field trip—Scavenger Hunt in hand—was the most fun our class ever had! It really brought the place and its history to life. They loved the real kids characters and all the humor. I loved seeing them learn that reading is an experience to enjoy!
—4th grade teacher

Carole Marsh is really on to something with these unique mysteries. They are so clever; kids want to read them all. The Teacher's Guides are chock full of activities, recipes, and additional fascinating information. My kids thought I was an expert on the subject—and with this tool, I felt like it!
—3rd grade teacher

My students loved writing their own Real Kids/Real Places mystery book! Ms. Marsh's reproducible guidelines are a real jewel. They learned about copyright and more & ended up with their own book they were so proud of!
—Reading/Writing Teacher

"The kids seem very realistic—my children seemed to relate to the characters. Also, it is educational by expanding their knowledge about the famous places in the books."

"They are what children like: mysteries and adventures with children they can relate to."

"Encourages reading for pleasure."

"This series is great. It can be used for reluctant readers, and as a history supplement."

The Mystery at

Mount Fuji

Tokyo, Japan

by Carole Marsh

Copyright ©2007 Carole Marsh/ Gallopade International
All rights reserved.
Second Printing November, 2008

Carole Marsh Mysteries™ and its skull colophon are the property of
Carole Marsh and Gallopade International.

Published by Gallopade International/Carole Marsh Books. Printed in the
United States of America.

Managing Editor: Sherry Moss
Senior Editor: Janice Baker
Assistant Editor: Fran Kramer
Cover Design: Vicki DeJoy
Content Design and Inside Illustrations: Yvonne Ford

The publisher would like to thank the following for their kind permission to
reproduce the cover photographs:

© **Hansen Atsuwara, image from BigStock Photo.com**
© **JupiterImages Corporation**

Gallopade International is introducing SAT words that kids need to know in each new book that
we publish. The SAT words are bold in the story. Look for this special logo beside
each word in the glossary. Happy Learning!

Gallopade is proud to be a member and supporter of these educational
organizations and associations:

American Booksellers Association
American Library Association
International Reading Association
National Association for Gifted Children
The National School Supply and Equipment Association
The National Council for the Social Studies
Museum Store Association
Association of Partners for Public Lands
Association of Booksellers for Children

This book is a complete work of fiction. All events are fictionalized, and although
the names of real people are used, their characterization in this book is fiction. All
attractions, product names, or other works mentioned in this book are trademarks
of their respective owners and the names and images used in this book are strictly
for editorial purposes; no commercial claims to their use is claimed by the author
or publisher.

Without limiting the rights under copyright reserved above, no part of this
publication may be reproduced, stored in or introduced into a retrieval system, or
transmitted, in any form or by any means (electronic, mechanical, photocopying,
recording or otherwise), without the prior written permission of both the copyright
owner and the above publisher of this book.

The scanning, uploading, and distribution of this book via the Internet or via any
other means without the permission of the publisher is illegal and punishable by
law. Please purchase only authorized electronic editions and do not participate in or
encourage electronic piracy of copyrightable materials. Your support of the author's
rights is appreciated.

30 Years Ago . . .

As a mother and an author, one of the fondest periods of my life was when I decided to write mystery books for children. At this time (1979) kids were pretty much glued to the TV, something parents and teachers complained about the same way they do about web surfing and video games today.

I decided to set each mystery in a real place—a place kids could go and visit for themselves after reading the book. And I also used real children as characters. Usually a couple of my own children served as characters, and I had no trouble recruiting kids from the book's location to also be characters.

Also, I wanted all the kids—boys and girls of all ages—to participate in solving the mystery. And, I wanted kids to learn something as they read. Something about the history of the location. And, I wanted the stories to be funny. That formula of real+scary+smart+fun served me well.

I love getting letters from teachers and parents who say they read the book with their class or child, then visited the historic site and saw all the places in the mystery for themselves. What's so great about that? What's great is that you and your children have an experience that bonds you together forever. Something you shared. Something you both cared about at the time. Something that crossed all age levels—a good story, a good scare, a good laugh!

30 years later,

Carole Marsh

Christina *Mimi* *Papa* *Grant*

"Mystery Girl"

Hey, kids! As you see—here we are ready to embark on another of our exciting Carole Marsh Mystery adventures! You know, in "real life," I keep very close tabs on Christina, Grant, and their friends when we travel. However, in the mystery books, they always seem to slip away from Papa and I so that they can try to solve the mystery on their own!

I hope you will go to www.carolemarshmysteries.com and apply to be a character in a future mystery book! Well, the *Mystery Girl* is all tuned up and ready for "take-off!"

Gotta go... Papa says so! Wonder what I've forgotten this time?

Happy "Armchair Travel" Reading,

Mimi

About the Characters

 **Christina**, age 10: Mysterious things really do happen to her! Hobbies: soccer, Girl Scouts, anything crafty, hanging out with Mimi, and going on new adventures.

 Grant, age 7: Always manages to fall off boats, back into cactuses, and find strange clues—even in real life! Hobbies: camping, baseball, computer games, math, and hanging out with Papa.

 **Mimi** is Carole Marsh, children's book author and creator of Carole Marsh Mysteries, Around the World in 80 Mysteries, Three Amigos Mysteries, Baby's First Mysteries, and many others.

 Papa is Bob Longmeyer, the author's real-life husband, who really does wear a tuxedo, cowboy boots and hat, fly an airplane, captain a boat, speak in a booming voice, and laugh a lot!

Travel around the world with Christina and Grant as they visit famous places in 80 countries, and experience the mysterious happenings that always seem to follow them!

Books in This Series

Table of Contents

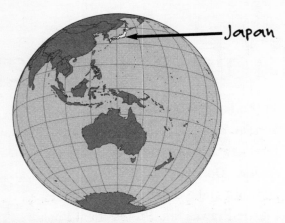

Japan

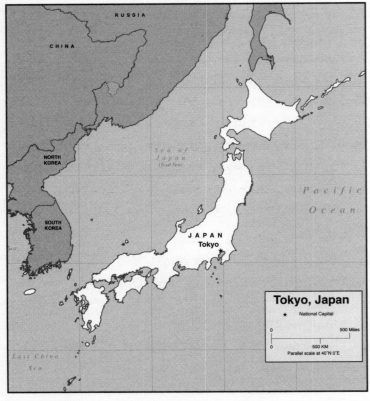

RUSSIA

CHINA

NORTH
KOREA

*Sea of
Japan
(East Sea)*

SOUTH
KOREA

JAPAN
Tokyo

*Pacific
Ocean*

Tokyo, Japan

★   National Capital

0   500 Miles

0   500 KM
Parallel scale at 40°N 0°E

*East China
Sea*

In the Land of the Rising Sun

"*Nihon*—what does that mean?" ten-year-old Christina tested Grant, her seven-year-old brother. "You should remember that from school a few days ago. Spring break's just started."

"Japan!" He crowed like a rooster. "That's easy. And look down there." Grant jabbed his finger against the airplane window. "Is that *Nihon* now?"

"Yep," Papa drawled as he stretched his long legs in the pilot's seat. "Those green hills are Japan. We'll be landing before you can say *Konnichi wa*."

"*Konnichi wa*! How are you? *Konnichi wa*! How are you?" Grant sang back, recalling a song he learned in school. Always the clown, he loved to perform for an audience. "But, Papa, we're not there yet."

"Oh yes, we are. Buckle your seat belts!" Papa said, as he turned off the automatic pilot, and banked the *Mystery Girl* for descent into Narita International Airport.

Pulling her long brown hair back from her eyes, Christina leaned over Grant to get her first look at Japan. "Thank heavens we're getting here," she said. "Japan is such a long way from home. My bottom hurts from sitting so long!"

"And my head hurts from you testing me so much about Japan!" Grant said, as he pushed her back from him. "I bet you were just trying to show off because you know so much, even how to write some of that funny Japanese writing. To me it looks a chicken left its tracks when it ran across the page."

"It is just like our handwriting, except our writing goes left to right and Japanese writing goes up and down," Christina explained. She ruffled her brother's hair, something he hated. Christina was proud that she had studied hard about Japan, and learned to write a few Japanese characters. Now she would see how much she learned!

Mimi, the children's grandmother, looked out the opposite window. "See the sunrise! Isn't it gorgeous?" she said.

A dazzling orange half ball of sun was edging up over the horizon, casting sharp rays of gold into the sky. While it filled the plane with yellow light, it cast dark shadows behind the hills below, making them look spooky.

"That must be why they call Japan the Land of the Rising Sun," Grant pondered. "No... I remember. It's because the Chinese thought the sun rose here when they named Japan *Nihon!*"

"Now, you're the one showing off," Christina teased. "But you're right, I have to say. The characters for Ni and Hon do mean the sun's source."

The bright April sun was up by the time the *Mystery Girl* was on the runway and taxiing to the hangar.

Meeting Christina, Grant, Mimi, and Papa inside the airport terminal was their host, Professor Kato. As president of a local mystery writers' association, he had invited Mimi, whose real name was Carole Marsh and whose job was writing children's mysteries, to speak to his organization. Mimi thought the invitation was very timely because the kids had recently learned so much about Japan and wanted to go there. So she accepted—and here they were, sore bottoms and all.

"*Mashu-san*!" Professor Kato exclaimed, smiling, as he came up to Mimi and bowed. The kids stared when they heard Mimi's last name pronounced in such an odd way. And their mouths dropped open when they saw Mimi slowly attempt a bow, looking like she didn't want to throw her back out of line.

"They really do bow here!" Grant said, surprised.

"And they say *San* instead of Mr. or Mrs," Christina whispered back.

Professor Kato was introduced to everyone in the group. When Grant met him, Professor Kato bowed slightly while Grant attempted a very deep, impressive bow that sent him tumbling!

Professor Kato laughed. He said to Mimi and Papa, "Your grandson knows that younger people bow more deeply to older people! He will do very well in Japan! We Japanese put a very strong emphasis on politeness."

Grant grinned and nudged Christina with his elbow, saying, "Betch'ya didn't think I would be known for my politeness?"

Christina rolled her eyes. Little brothers could get to you sometimes—especially after being cooped up with one on a plane for so long! "No," she agreed, "Just your clumsiness."

"My granddaughter rolls her eyes at her brother, too," Professor Kato said. "That is truly a universal expression. I think sisters do that everywhere to their brothers. By the way, tomorrow, I will bring my grandchildren to meet you. Taro is my grandson and Mitsuki is my granddaughter. They are near your ages. They would love to show you the sights."

"Wow! Our own tour guides!" Grant cried with relief. He was already noticing how many signs in the airport were in that funny writing. And he couldn't read them backward or forward! He suddenly felt like a very little kid again, not knowing anything.

Grant saw that Christina was also eyeing all the strange signs. "We will need some guides," Christina said. "Japan is one big mystery, even if we think we know something about it."

Professor Kato saw their anxious looks, and said to comfort them, "Japan is a strange place to foreigners. It will be our pleasure to help you unravel its mystery!"

At that time, little did Christina and Grant know that Japan's mysteries would take so many forms—*and bring them so much danger!*

A Yen for Yen

Professor Kato said he would take them to their hotel after he had arranged to pick up their baggage.

"Where are we staying?" Grant asked. "Are we going to sleep on the floor? People sleeping on floors in Japan—I saw that in a movie!"

"I am sorry, *Garanta-kun*," Professor Kato politely apologized, using the Japanese form of Grant's name. "Tonight you will sleep in a bed in a Western-style hotel. But don't worry. You will sleep on *tatami* before you leave Japan."

"*Tatami*, the mats on the floor—I know that word!" Grant replied. His face lit up like the rising sun. It really did make you feel good to know a little about a place before you got there.

Professor Kato asked Mimi and the kids to wait in the airport lounge while he and Papa left to see about the baggage. The room was large, and filled with people coming and going on their journeys. Along the walls were displays of handmade art objects and electronic products made in Japan, inviting the newly-arrived tourists to explore the many wonders of the country. Mimi stopped to look at a fabulous flower arrangement.

From a distance, Grant spied a large glass display case filled with pictures of some of the fattest men he had ever seen—wearing nothing but loincloths. They were wrestling in a big arena.

"Sumo players!" Grant yelled to Christina. "Let's go over and look." Pushing his way through a crowd of arriving travelers, Grant made a beeline for the display case. Christina, scared she would lose him in the throng, bolted after him.

Reaching the sumo display case, Grant pressed his nose against the glass to get a good view. He could now see inside the whole case. "Cooool," he said, as his eyes were drawn to the bottom of the display where he spotted a gleaming Japanese short sword, mounted on a red lacquer stand. The hilt was made of gold, with Japanese characters engraved on it. The silver blade was so shiny the light danced off it.

Christina also marveled at the curved, sharp blade with its red silk tassel. She stood on her toes to read the sign above it, written in English for the tourists. "The sign says the sword was a gift to a famous sumo Grand Champion from the Emperor of Japan."

"That's so cool!" Grant whispered to Christina.

At that moment, Christina heard another whisper behind her. It was a truly wicked whisper, saying, "That sword is worth a ton of *yen,* and I know a rich man in Hong Kong who would gladly pay big money for something like it!"

Warily, Christina turned around. She saw a short, brown-haired man staring at the sword. He muttered something else that Christina couldn't understand. Then the man realized he was being noticed. He shot Christina a nasty look, and slinked off into the crowd.

"Who is that guy?" Grant asked. "Boy, he gave you a dirty look!"

Christina shuddered. She felt the hairs on the back of her neck stand up. "I don't know," she said. "I wouldn't want to run into him in a dark alley in Tokyo!" But as he walked off, she had a weird feeling their paths would cross again. She couldn't help but notice he was wearing a black leather motorcycle jacket with the characters for Japan—*Nihon*—embroidered in gold on the back.

Christina was glad to see Papa and Professor Kato return to take them to the hotel.

After a long car ride into Tokyo, the group was soon checked into the hotel. As Professor Kato said, it was Western style, a gleaming skyscraper, made of steel and concrete. But the rooms were homey and comfortable. Professor

Kato left his guests to freshen up. He would meet them later at the restaurant downstairs.

Christina, Grant, Mimi, and Papa began unpacking and getting ready for lunch.

Mimi said to Papa, "When you were getting the hotel rooms, I took a look at the prices in the gift shop and restaurant. Nothing is cheap around here."

Papa said, "It's pricey all right. I heard you can pay ten bucks for a cup of coffee. That's a lot of dollars for coffee, or I should say, a lot of *yen*!"

Grant looked at his grandfather. "Papa, ten dollars is our whole allowance! I don't want to buy a cup of coffee. Can you help me out?" he pleaded. "I have a yen for *yen* right now!"

Christina chimed in, knowing Papa had a soft heart and could be easily persuaded. "Ten dollars will only buy comics and candy here. Could you help us, please?"

"Ok, ok," Papa said, pulling some *yen* from his jeans pocket. "I'd rather you buy something besides comics and candy."

Soon it was time to meet Professor Kato for lunch. He was waiting for them at the restaurant door. Grant skipped up to him and said, "I'm starved! Are we...uh...going to eat seaweed? I heard the Japanese like to eat seaweed."

"No, not right now," Professor Kato said, and laughed. "I bet some *teriyaki* chicken sounds more delicious. What do you think?"

"*Teriyaki* is great! My mom makes that sometimes," said Grant.

"*Teriyaki* it is then," Professor Kato said as he walked through the door. "Shall we go eat?"

Professor Kato showed Christina and Grant to their table, which looked like a table in any American restaurant with silverware, plates and napkins, except there appeared to be two napkins for each person. One was warm, damp, and neatly rolled up.

"Why do we have two napkins?" Grant asked. "Is the meal really messy? I might need two napkins if I use chopsticks!"

"No," Professor Kato said, laughing. "The wet cloth is an *oshiburi*. You use it like a wash cloth to wipe off your hands before you eat."

Just after the kids sat down and wiped their hands with the little wet towels, two Japanese kids in dark blue school uniforms peeked into the restaurant.

"Taro-*kun*! Mitsuki-*chan*!" Professor Kato called out. "Come meet your guests!"

Professor Kato introduced the children to Mimi and Papa, and then to Christina and Grant. Taro was a serious boy of eleven, with glasses and a crew cut.

"Taro loves electronics," Professor Kato said. "Please don't let him bore you with all his talk about computers and other gadgets. He is a real—how do you say it—'geek'? And Mitsuki..." he indicated the pretty, round-faced girl who stood next to him. "Mitsuki makes some attempts at drawing and painting. She also tries her hand at writing. My grandchildren are nothing much to brag about—but they try hard. Also, please excuse their poor English."

Christina was stunned to hear Professor Kato talk about his grandchildren this way. He really seemed to love them, yet from his words, he didn't seem very proud of them. Or, who knows, maybe they just weren't the brightest kids around? Or perhaps, she thought to herself, there is something here I don't understand—a puzzle to solve!

Christina soon found out that any American parent would love to brag about kids like Taro and Mitsuki. She discovered they were simply amazing. Their English turned out to be excellent, despite what their grandfather said. How did they speak English so well—in addition to Japanese?

Over steaming plates of *teriyaki* chicken and rice, Christina's curiosity got the better of her as she began asking the two Japanese kids questions, one after another. At first, the kids were a little slow to talk.

"Don't mind her," Grant said. "Christina's always trying to find out about things and people. She loves to solve puzzles, and you're a mystery to her!"

Taro laughed and said, "Ok. We just don't want to bore you. If you really do want to know..." And off he launched like a rocket from the pad, telling Christina and Grant about himself and his sister. As to why they spoke English well, he said, "Mitsuki and I go to an international school in Yokohama. We learn both English and Japanese. Our parents think that nowadays it is very important to know more than one language."

Christina leaned over to Mitsuki and asked, "How come your grandfather thinks you don't speak English well? You sound like an American!"

Mitsuki laughed. "That is one of the mysteries of how we speak," she said. "Grandfather is only saying that to be polite. And maybe to give you a pleasant surprise. Also, if we do make mistakes in English, you won't be disappointed."

"And is that why he didn't exactly praise you and Taro?" asked Christina.

"Oh, yes," Taro chimed in. "We think it is rude to brag about one's family. Don't worry. We know he thinks the world of us."

"You're so lucky," Christina said, just a tiny bit jealous of her new friends' experience and abilities. "You can live in two worlds, not just one! Can you read and write in two languages, too?"

"Oh, yes," Mitsuki said. "But for our grade level only. It takes Japanese kids a long time to learn all the characters we call *kanji*. There are thousands of them."

"Can you teach me to write my name in Japanese?" Grant asked.

"Sure, one of these days I will. That's fun and easy. You'll see," Mitsuki said.

Taro chimed in, "And we have all sorts of other fun things planned."

Just as the kids were finishing their meal, some American tourists at the next table got up to leave. The woman put down some cash on the table. "This is for the tip," she said to her friend, and left.

In an instant, a small man seemed to slide from out of nowhere. With one swoop of his hand, he scooped up the tip money.

Grant was shocked. He yelled, "Hey, you shouldn't do that!"

"There's no tipping in Japan, kid. The waitress won't even miss it," he snarled, laughing as he stuffed the money in his pocket. Then he saw Christina. Like a vicious dog, he snapped at her, saying, "You again! You...you better stay out of my way!" He then slinked out of the restaurant.

"You've seen him before?" Taro asked.

Christina put her hand to her face, not believing what she just saw and heard. "It's the weird guy I saw in the airport! He was standing behind me when Grant and I were looking at a *samurai* sword in a display case. He said something really strange." Christina put her hands under her chin, trying to recall his exact words.

"What did he say?" Mitsuki asked.

"Well, I think he was talking out loud to himself," said Christina. "He said something about that sword being worth a lot of *yen*, and that he knew somebody who would be willing to pay anything to get it. I wonder what he meant?"

"That is a strange thing to say," Mitsuki said. "From those words, I wouldn't know what he meant either, but one thing is for sure. He is a **callous** guy. He doesn't care about people's feelings."

"He is slick," Taro said. "Did you see the way he lifted that money—like a vacuum cleaner!"

Christina had been right—she had encountered the man again, sooner than she ever expected. He was a most unsavory character, and she hoped their paths never crossed a third time. Surely they would not?

Lost in a Maze

"That sword we saw at the airport was really neat," Grant said, wanting to get his mind off the rude man.

"Would you like to go a sword museum?" Taro asked. "I know where there is one, right here in Tokyo."

"Wow! That would be great," Grant said. "How about you, Christina?"

"Oh, I think I'd like it," Christina answered. "If you guys don't take forever going through the museum and if we girls get dibs on choosing the next place to go."

"Boys go first in Japan," Mitsuki said. "This time we will act like Japanese and let them have their way."

"I will tell Grandfather our plan," Taro said as he got up to go to the adults' table. Taro briefly told Professor Kato where he would take his young guests.

"That would be fun for them," Professor Kato said to Mimi and Papa. "And something to occupy their time while we discuss your talk for the mystery writers' club. You needn't worry. Japan is a very safe place for kids to run about on their own. My grandson has learned his way around Tokyo. He goes everywhere by himself."

The kids were soon bounding down the streets, fascinated by the exotic smells and sights. Taro led the way as they scampered down some steps and boarded a subway. The subway trains, which were very clean and shiny, arrived every few minutes. In no time, they were at the sword museum.

"Getting around seems so easy here," Christina said. "You don't need a car."

"If you know where you are going, and can read the signs, it is," Taro agreed. Inside the museum, Taro again led the way and acted as tour guide.

"The *samurai* carried two swords," Taro said. "I bet you know who the *samurai* were, don't you, Grant?"

"The warriors of old Japan!" Grant said. He

squatted down and held out both arms rigidly, as if holding a sword in each hand. "But why did they have two swords? One of those things would be enough to slice somebody into lunch meat!"

Taro laughed. "The long sword was for fighting. The short sword was for backup in case something happened to the long sword in a fight. And it had another purpose. In the old days, the *samurai* used it to kill himself--if he had to in a very desperate situation."

"Why would he kill himself?" Grant asked, appalled. He couldn't imagine anyone would want to do something like that.

"That was the way of the Japanese warrior,"

Taro answered. "If the *samurai* lost a fight, his honor demanded he kill himself. It would be too shameful to surrender. His family would be scorned by everybody. When a *samurai* killed himself this way, it was done very seriously with ritual and ceremony. We call it *hara-kiri*. In English, Americans call it hari-kari."

"That must have made them very fierce fighters," Grant said.

The kids explored the museum, poring over the many elaborate swords on display. Some were ancient. All were very beautiful, and quite deadly with their curved, razor-sharp blades.

"Do you think some of these swords were used to kill people?" Grant asked, feeling spooked at all this talk of death.

"I am sure some were," Taro said. "But I like them because they are some of the best swords in the world. It takes real skill and patience to make them. The sword-maker must repeat a process of heating a layer of metal, then folding it and beating it many times. There can be over 30,000 layers of steel in one sword."

"Wow!" Grant said, awed by the time and patience required to make a real *samurai* sword.

The girls were not so impressed. "Hey guys," Christina said, trying to move them along. "There's a museum gift shop. Let's see what they have to sell."

In addition to imitation and toy *samurai* swords, the shop sold a variety of traditional Japanese things which caught the girls' eyes, such as *origami* paper and dolls. The girls checked out the *origami* paper while the boys looked over the swords.

"Hey, Christina," Grant called to his sister. "This sword looks exactly like the one we saw at the airport."

Christina came over to look. "Boy, it sure does! It even has the same red tassel."

In Japanese, Taro asked the clerk about the sword. The clerk said that all the kids and even adults wanted a sword just like the sword given to the sumo Grand Champion by the emperor of Japan. This was a superb imitation—very much like a real *samurai* sword! Also, it was not cheap. Taro explained this to Grant in English.

"That explains why it looks the same," said Christina.

"Taro, I want to buy one for Papa," Grant said. "Please tell the man I want to buy one."

"I don't know," Christina said. "I wonder if Papa would really want a sword. He's not big on weapons. And it looks too much like the real thing to me."

"No, the blade's not as sharp as the real thing," Taro said. "Grant won't hurt anybody with that."

"I'm not worried about him hurting someone else," Christina said. "I'm afraid he will get hurt!"

"Why do you say that?" Mitsuki asked.

"I don't know," Christina said. "Maybe it's just a feeling I have."

"Oh, come on, Christina," Grant griped. "You worry too much!"

"Well, ok," Christina said, wondering if she was doing the right thing.

Grant bought the sword. The clerk put it in a box and slid the box into a big shopping bag.

They left the museum, and found that the streets were getting very crowded. Christina, Grant, Taro, and Mitsuki now had to push their way through the throngs of Japanese.

Mitsuki said, "This is Tokyo *Rashu Owa.* You call it 'rush hour.' Everybody is leaving work. We have to stick together or we'll lose each other."

With one hand, Grant hung on to Christina's arm. With the other, he clutched the shopping bag. People were now very close, surging around them. The kids felt like they were floating in a whitewater raft, pushed along by a strong current.

Suddenly, Grant felt a jerk on his shopping bag, as if someone was trying to snatch it away from him. He tugged the bag to his chest and could tell it was now empty!

"Stop! Christina, Taro!" Grant yelled.

The kids gathered around him. Grant yanked the bag open and peered inside. He swatted through the tissue paper. "Papa's sword is gone!" he wailed. "Someone stole it!"

Taro said, "Maybe it just fell out in the jostling crowd. Let's look for the sword. But stick together—I don't want anyone to get lost."

Like salmon swimming upstream, the kids retraced their steps. Squirming through the maze of people on the street, the kids looked for the sword box, but couldn't find it.

Christina looked back inside the shopping bag and pulled out the receipt. A second piece of paper fluttered out with it. "What's this?" she asked.

The kids drew close, and Christina read:

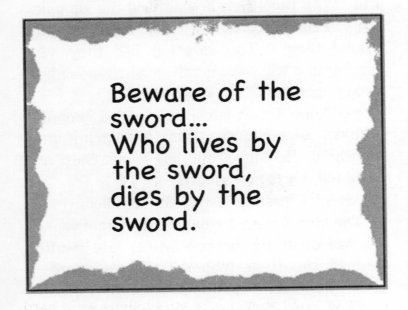

Beware of the
sword...
Who lives by
the sword,
dies by the
sword.

"What's that supposed to mean?" asked
Grant, near tears. "It sounds like a threat from
the thief!"

*The other kids stared at each other and
shrugged their shoulders. They all were in a
confused maze—and it wasn't just from the crowd of
people around them!*

A New "Do" Will Do It!

"I don't like this. Let's get out of the crowd," Taro said as he led the kids down a side street to escape the throng. But soon they were lost in a maze of small alleys. The street signs were hard to decipher, even for Taro and Mitsuki, who did not recognize some of the *kanji*.

An old man pushing a bicycle seemed to be following the kids. His bicycle was piled high with noodle bowls stacked in a rack behind the seat. There were odd sacks filled with strange contents attached to the sides of his bike.

The old man seemed friendly so Mitsuki decided to ask him for directions. He parked his bike and wiped his face with the end of a white towel he had tied around his head. He not only told the kids how to get to the hotel, but took a piece of paper from Mitsuki and drew a beautiful map. While drawing the map, he asked the kids many questions, like what they were doing and why they visited the sword museum. Christina couldn't help but wonder if he was just being chatty or if there was another reason for his talk. One box peeking out of a sack on the bike looked oddly familiar—like the sword box! "Am I imagining things?" she asked herself.

Back in the quiet haven of the hotel lobby, the kids met the adults and told them about the missing sword. Grant was angry with himself for losing such a valuable gift he had bought for Papa.

Papa tried to comfort Grant. "Don't be too upset," he said. "This was something you couldn't do anything about. Sometimes things like this just happen."

Taro felt bad about the theft from his friend. He apologized to Grant. "*Sumimasen*. I'll go back to the museum. I will help you get your sword back!"

"You don't have to do that," Christina said. "It wasn't your fault."

"But it is," Taro insisted. "I should have been more careful in that crowd."

Mitsuki said, "We should go back to the sword museum, anyway. The museum gift shop's name was written on the box. Whoever found it will probably return it to the shop. That's the Japanese way."

Christina thought Mitsuki was just trying to comfort them. In the crowd, it would be easy to grab the sword box from the shopping bag. The sword was an expensive replica. Why would anyone want to return it if they stole it? Then there was the note. Why would anybody want to scare kids with a note like that?

Mitsuki saw concern on Christina's face. "Don't worry," she said. "Let's go and have some fun. Japan is really a great place, especially for kids. Let's meet tomorrow and go shopping! The guys can do whatever they want to do."

The next morning, Mitsuki was waiting in the hotel lobby to pick up Christina. "What do you want do?" she asked.

"I want to buy a Japanese robe. I think you call it a *kimono*. Do you have one?" Christina asked her friend as they left the hotel. "I've only seen you wear your school uniform."

"Oh yes, I wear a *kimono* for special occasions," Mitsuki replied. "Like Girls' Day and Boys' Day. Those are special days for children."

"Girls' Day? You mean you have a fun day just for girls?" Christina asked.

"Yes. Just as you have Mother's Day and Father's Day, we have Girls' Day," said Mitsuki. "We also call it the Doll Festival. It's on March 3. I wear my *kimono*, and my mother helps me set up my collection of dolls in a special place in the house. Then my family prays I will have a good future."

"Cool," said Christina. "And the boys? Do they have their day?"

"Sure," said Mitsuki. "It's on May 5. We also call it Children's Day because girls join in. I help Taro celebrate. We set up a collection of his toy swords and *samurai* helmets. Taro also has some *samurai* dolls we display. We pray and honor our ancestors."

"The fun part," she continued, "is that we also hang up banners in front of our house. The banners are made in the shape of a fish. There's one banner for each boy in the family. We have one hanging right now for Taro because May 5 is coming soon!"

"I really want a *kimono*," Christina said. "But we don't have all those holidays. When would I wear it?"

"Oh, you could wear it soon!" said Mitsuki. "There will be a cherry blossom festival in a few days. That would be a great time to wear a *kimono*."

The girls arrived at a big department store called Mitsukoshi. It was famous for selling *kimono*s. Mitsuki took Christina in hand as they looked over the colorful selection of Japanese robes.

"We need to get you a bright *kimono*," Mitsuki said. "Young women and girls wear bright colors, like pink and red. Middle aged women wear colors like tan, dark green, and blue. Very old ladies wear browns and blacks."

After Christina tried on several *kimono*s, she bought a pale pink one with small red and yellow flowers dotted on the sleeves and hem. She also chose a red and yellow checked belt to go with it.

"The belt is called an *obi*," Mitsuki said. "I will help you put it on. It's not easy to tie. Oh, let's not forget your feet!"

Mitsuki led Christina to another department where they found white socks called *tabi*.

"These socks have a split between the big and next toe so you can wear the *geta*," Mitsuki explained, as she headed to the shoe department.

"The what-a?" Christina asked.

"Geta," Mitsuki said as she showed Christina a pair of wooden clogs with a strap between the toes.

"I like the ones with the red strap," Christina said. "Don't you think they will go with the *kimono*?" she asked, sliding her foot into the clog.

Mitsuki reached into the shopping bag and compared the cloth of the *kimono* to the shoe strap. "It's a perfect match!" she said, smiling.

The girls left the store, very happy with their shopping trip.

On the way back to the hotel, Christina said, "Mimi, my grandmother, wants to get her hair cut. I need a haircut, too. Can you come with us? You've been such a big help."

"Japanese hair cutters would love to cut your hair," Mitsuki said. "It is so different from ours. You'll see!"

The girls hurried back to the hotel to get Mimi. Mitsuki led Mimi and Christina to a beauty parlor down the street. As soon as they entered, they were surrounded by the manager and the hair dressers, who stared at Mimi's and Christina's hair.

Mitsuki explained the commotion. "They have only cut and styled the straight, thick black hair of Japanese people," she said. "It will be new for them to work with your grandmother's blonde, curly hair. And your brown hair—the texture is finer and more delicate."

Sure enough, when Mimi and Christina were seated, several hair dressers gathered around each chair to listen to the manager explain how to cut Mimi's and Christina's hair.

Christina was a little nervous about her haircut. Mitsuki's smiling face calmed her. She took a deep breath and said, "Mitsuki, please tell the hairdresser I just want a new short hairdo, a little over the ears—not as short as a boy's haircut, but almost."

Little did Christina know that her new hairdo would cause her big problems!

A Sword and a Sony

While the girls shopped, Taro took Grant back to the sword museum to see if the sword had been returned.

"*Sumimasen*," the manager said. "I am very sorry. No one has returned a sword."

Grant decided to buy more gifts for his family. He thought of *origami* paper for Christina. He knew she would like it because in school she had learned how to make cranes and frogs by folding the *origami* paper in intricate ways. Taro asked the manager if they could leave the bag by the cash register while they looked at other gifts in the store.

Grant went to buy a gold silk scarf embroidered with dragons for Mimi and a very nice writing pen for Papa.

After all the gifts were purchased, Taro asked Grant if there was something he wanted.

Grant thought a moment and said, "I want to get a digital camera, one of those small ones you can put in your pocket." He held up his hands and moved his fingers, pretending to snap a picture of Taro.

"I know just where to go, Grant," Taro said. "There's a place called Akihabara where the tiny shops are crammed full of all the latest equipment like computers, cell phones, and DVD players. We can find a camera there." He added, "I always go to Akihabara because I really like electronic gadgets. Sometimes I buy something like a radio just to bring it home and take it apart. I like to see what's inside and find out how it works."

On the train to Akihabara, Grant asked Taro about his name. "Does it have a meaning? Or is it just a name?"

Taro laughed and said, "It means 'great son.' I guess it was one way my mom and dad could say how great I was and they were glad I was born."

"Great son, how are you?" Grant asked, and giggled.

"You're right, Grant," said Taro. "It sounds silly in English."

"How about Sonny?" Grant asked. "Kids get called that in America all the time."

"That sounds too American," Taro said.

"Then how about Sony?" said Grant. "Sony is Japanese. It seems like so many electronic things in Japan are made by Sony. You like electronics and you were made in Japan."

Taro laughed. "You can call me Sony if you want. It certainly fits," he said, smiling.

From that point on, Grant called Taro "Sony."

Taro and Grant arrived in Akihabara, a bustling, crowded neighborhood filled with small and large stores. Each store was trying to outsell the other in every kind of electronic appliance, gadget and device imaginable. Everywhere they went, Taro was greeted by the sales people. They all seemed to know him, and jumped to offer assistance when the kids came into the store.

It wasn't long before Grant found the camera he wanted. It fit exactly in his small hand. "It will also fit in my pocket," he said. "And look, Sony. It's a Sony!"

The boys headed back to the hotel to meet up with the girls. All the kids came to Christina's room where they showed one another what they had bought. With Taro's help, Grant opened his camera box and began charging the battery so he could take pictures.

Then Grant reached into the bag to give Christina her *origami* paper. As he did so, he noticed another piece of *origami* paper lying loose.

"What's this?" Grant cried. "This *origami* paper is all bent up. I bought only good paper, Christina."

Christina's heart skipped a beat when she saw it. There was some writing on the back of the wrinkled paper. One of the four corners of the paper was cut off. The kids all looked at each other.

"Another note?" Mitsuki asked, a little worried.

"It looks like it," Christina said. She read:

Beware! Stay
away from
swords.

See the crane's
neck.

Mitsuki asked, "The crane's neck? What does that mean?"

Christina started folding the *origami* paper along the wrinkle lines. It formed a crane! Her heart sank when she saw the cut was along the corner that was meant for the crane's neck.

Grant was angry. Why would someone write a note like that? And why was the note put in his bag? He put down his camera and hugged Christina. *Little did he know that his camera would come in handy later—in a strange way.*

Plastic Prawns and Professional Pushers

After the second note showed up, Mitsuki and Taro wanted Christina and Grant to have some real fun more than ever. It was time to ride the trains and see the sights! Grant proudly took his new camera with him.

"Sony says we should see the Imperial Palace—that's where the emperor lives!" Grant told Christina. Christina looked confused. She said, "Sony, who's Sony?"

"Oh, that's my name for Taro," he said. He then told Christina why he gave Taro that special nickname.

"It is a good nickname," Christina agreed.

"Well, I guess I am Sony to Grant," Taro said, shaking his head.

The kids headed to the Imperial Palace. They walked along the street next to the palace moat, a deep stone embankment filled with water. They gazed at the exotic palace, made up of large white buildings with gray tile roofs that curled up at the ends. A stone bridge over the moat led the way into the palace.

Taro pointed to the bridge and said, "That's the Nijubashi Bridge. It was built in 1888, but a palace was first built here a long time ago, in the 1500s. It was expanded over the years. What we see now has mostly been fixed up since World War II because parts of the palace were destroyed in the war."

Grant took a picture of Christina and his Japanese friends with the bridge in the background. Then he asked Taro, "Can we go in?"

"*Sumimasen*, Grant," Taro said. "People can only go inside at the New Year's holiday and on the emperor's birthday."

"To help him celebrate his birthday?" Grant asked. Grant loved birthday parties.

"Yes," Taro said, "something like that. But you just can't drop in and say 'Hi, Happy Birthday.' In the old days before the war, the Japanese thought the emperor was **divine**, a real god. Even now, many Japanese would feel very shy in front of him. So on his birthday, there is a special event at the palace where he can meet the people."

From the Imperial Palace, they took a subway to the Senso-ji Temple. This was a large and very popular Buddhist temple with many gardens around it. They wandered through a garden filled with bamboo trees and arrived at some large red wooden buildings with gray tile roofs. One building was tall and thin. Standing above the others, it had five stories with a curved roof jutting out at each level. Mitsuki called it a *pagoda*. Near the *pagoda*, the kids saw a huge metal pot with smoke pouring out. People of all ages crowded around it.

"What are they doing?" Christina asked.

"That's an incense burner," Mitsuki said. "People think that the burning incense smoke will make them healthy if it blows on them."

Nearby, people clapped their hands together and prayed, or tossed coins into a large wooden box bigger than a trunk.

Grant said, "When we go to church, a man passes around a plate and people put money it. With that big box, the monks can collect a fortune!"

Christina laughed, and said, "And it looks like they don't have to wait till Sunday to get it."

Mitsuki agreed. "People come here every day to pray and give money."

The children then explored a long narrow passageway that led to a very large red gate with a heavy tiled roof. Taro called it "Thunder Gate." The gate was protected by two fierce warrior gods, one on each side. It was a popular place for picture-taking. Grant asked Taro to take his picture in front of one of the warrior god statues. He struck a fierce fighting pose, trying hard to **emulate** a warrior god.

Taro yelled, "Stay in that pose! Some Japanese people want to take *your* picture!"

Grant was happy to please, and stuck out his scrawny seven-year-old chest even further. He knitted his eyebrows, made a ferocious frown, and pretended he was holding a sword.

At that moment, flash bulbs suddenly went off all over in front of him. A crowd of kids and parents had gathered to watch. Grant made a deep bow, and everyone clapped.

After the crowd melted away, Taro asked his friends if they were hungry. "Now is your chance to eat just like us Japanese," he said.

"This is going to be fun," Christina told Mitsuki. "But, I don't know if Grant and I are ready to eat raw fish."

"Do you eat the fish tails, too?" Grant asked, swallowing hard and wondering what eating raw fish would be like.

"Sometimes. But for today we can eat fish cooked, if you like," Mitsuki said. "I know some of our food takes some getting used to. How about some shrimp and vegetables cooked in noodles?" Mitsuki asked.

"That sounds a lot like vegetable soup at home. We love that," Christina said.

Taro led the way to a nearby noodle shop. Inside the shop, there were the usual tables for the customers but nearby there were also several tables covered with food. Taro picked up a piece of shrimp. "Grant, check this out," he said as he put the shrimp in front of Grant's face. As Grant moved closer to get a better look at it, he opened his mouth.

"Grant, stop, don't eat it!" Mitsuki pleaded.

"I wasn't really going to eat it," Grant protested. "We haven't paid for it."

Mitsuki giggled, and said, "That's not the only reason why you can't eat it. It's not real!"

"What?" Grant asked. He grabbed the shrimp with his fingers and found out, sure enough, it was made of plastic. "Boy, it looks real—and delicious," he said. "But it's a real fake."

"It's plastic," Taro agreed. "The noodle shop displays them so that the people eating here will know what's in the dish they are ordering."

Before feasting on noodle soup, Grant needed a lesson in using chopsticks. "Hold one chopstick between your thumb and middle finger like this," Taro said as he put the wooden stick between Grant's fingers. "Then press your thumb next to the middle finger to anchor the stick. It stays put and doesn't move." Taro took the other chopstick and put it between the ends of Grant's thumb and forefinger. "This stick acts as the lever," he said. "You move it back and forth against the tip of the other stick to grab the food."

Grant stared at the sticks in his hand. Slowly, he tried clicking the end of the sticks together. He finally got his chopsticks around a piece of shrimp. "It works!" he yelled, as he lifted the shrimp to his mouth.

The kids dug into the food. It was fun sucking the long slippery noodles into their mouths.

"My mother would have a fit if she saw us slurping food like this," Christina said.

"Here in Japan, it's ok to make noise eating your noodles," Taro replied. "It lets the cook know you enjoy the food!"

Grant puckered his cheeks and sucked a big wet noodle into his mouth.

Taro laughed and said, "I bet the chef heard that all the way in the kitchen!"

The trip home proved to be another scary adventure during rush hour. Along with the flashing neon lights, strange writing, honking horns and hawking peddlers on the narrow streets, the kids encountered a surging wave of office workers pouring through the streets. But this time they knew how to hang on to each other, and stuck together like links in a chain.

The kids bored through the crowd to get to the station. On the train platform, they were shoved to and fro as mobs of people rushed to get through the opening train doors. Christina felt a heavy push from behind but landed neatly inside the train car. Taro caught her arm to steady her. She turned around to see a man in a blue suit and white gloves pushing a young man behind her.

"That's a professional pusher," Mitsuki said, as she pulled Christina further into the train. "His job is to push people onto trains."

"I could do that job," said Grant, as the electric doors slammed shut. "Mimi says I'm pushy sometimes."

Just then, Taro found a tiny empty space in the corner, and the kids huddled together. Christina reached into her pocket to get a piece of gum. Instead, she found something else. She pulled out a ragged piece of paper.

"Somebody else must have pushed me, too," she said. "Look what I just found in my pocket!"

She showed the kids another note. She read:

Beware,
don't push me
too far.

Stables—But Not for Horses!

The next morning, Grant asked Taro if he could take them to see a sumo match. He was fascinated by the pictures of sumo players he had seen at the airport.

"The tournaments don't start until next month," Taro said. "But I know where we can go to see sumo players. How about that?"

"Awesome," Grant shouted. "Where are we going?"

"To the stables," Taro said.

"Do sumo players ride horses?" Grant asked. "It would be weird to see one of those big fat men on top of a horse, with hardly any clothes on!"

"Sumo players don't often ride horses," Taro said. "We call the building where the sumo players live and train a stable. There's a stable not so far from here. Does everyone want to go?"

Everyone said, "Yes!" As the children approached the sumo training hall, they saw brightly decorated banners flying merrily in the breeze.

"The names of the sumo players belonging to this stable are written on the banners," Taro explained. "One of the sumo players is now a Grand Champion. He won the tournament last year. He's very famous in Japan."

Grant said, "Just like in our country when a baseball player hits a lot of home runs, everyone knows his name."

The kids went through the main gate and entered the hall. They took off their shoes at the door and placed them in little cubbyholes lined up against the wall.

"Put on these slippers," Taro whispered, as he handed the kids some adult-size terry cloth slippers. "We have to be quiet so we don't disturb the wrestlers."

"Why do we have to put on these slippers?" Grant whispered. "Are we going to take a bath?"

"No," said Taro, "in Japanese houses, guests are given slippers so they don't have to go barefoot or get their socks dirty."

The slippers were way too big for all the kids. Even though they tried to tiptoe on the polished wood floors, they sounded like geese flapping their wings as they padded down the hallway.

Taro led them into the training room. They took seats alongside what looked like a boxing ring except it was covered with sand. Soon, two huge men waddled out. They were wearing nothing but white loincloths. Their hair was long, and tied in a single knot on the top of their heads.

Each player took a corner of the ring, opposite the other. They warmed up by lifting one leg very high and then swinging the leg heavily down, making a loud thud as the foot hit the ground. The wrestlers repeated the step with the other leg. Then they walked slowly around the stage, eyeing one another. Sometimes they gave a menacing look to someone in the audience. They were fearsome!

Taro whispered to Grant, "As long as a sumo player belongs to the stable and is playing like a pro, he has to wear that hairstyle. If you see a big man on the street wearing normal clothes, and he has that hairstyle, you know he's a sumo player."

Soon the men closed in on each other. Each one tried to knock the other out of the ring with pulls, grabs and throws. At last, one succeeded, and sent the other rolling out of the ring.

Suddenly, the kids heard a loud commotion. Taro led the other kids to where a crowd was gathering in the trophy room. He asked a man standing nearby what was happening. Then he turned to Christina, Grant, and Mitsuki and said, "The Grand Champion himself is coming in a few minutes. He's going to present his sword to the sumo stable for display!"

"Do you think that's the same sword we saw at the airport?" Christina asked the other kids.

"Let's wait and see," Taro said.

Soon a black limousine pulled up to the front gate. A huge Japanese man wearing a gray *kimono* and *geta* and carrying a long narrow box wrapped in gray silk got out of the car. He was met with cheers as he entered the trophy room.

A short ceremony began. The stable manager thanked the sumo player for the sword.

The sumo player opened the box so all could see the sword inside. Then, he bowed and handed the box to the sumo stable manager who placed it on a table nearby. Everyone, especially the kids, gathered round to see the Grand Champion and the sword. Taro, Mitsuki, Christina and Grant lined up to greet him, part of a long line moving past the table where the sword was placed.

As they neared the table with the sword, they got to see it up close.

Christina said, "It's the same one we saw at the airport! The one that was a gift from the emperor!"

Grant said, "It looks just like the one I bought for Papa!"

When they moved up in line to greet the sumo player, all the kids bowed to the Grand Champion. Grant piped up, "*Konnichi wa*! How are you?"

The sumo player laughed. He reached out his massive arm to shake Grant's hand.

"Wow!" Grant said, with a grin as big as the sumo player's. He shyly held out his hand. The sumo player completely wrapped Grant's little hand in his big one.

"*Konnichi wa*," said the Grand Champion. He then took Christina's hand and shook it also.

The kids hurried out of the sumo stable, bursting with excitement over their encounter with the famous sumo player. "I can't wait to tell Mimi and Papa!" cried Grant.

"You sure are lucky!" Taro said. "All the kids in Japan would be jealous of you. You got to shake the hand of the Grand Champion."

As they were walking toward the train station to go home, they heard a loud, eerie "wa-wa-wa" sound coming from the direction of the sumo stable.

"What's that?" Grant asked.

"A police siren," Mitsuki said. "Somebody must have called the police."

Christina felt the hairs on the back of her neck stand up and wondered why.

Under the Pink Clouds

When Mimi saw Christina take the new *kimono* out of the closet, she asked, "Where are you off to today? Is there something special?"

"Oh yes, Mimi," Christina answered. "We are going to a cherry blossom festival. Mitsuki told me to wear my new *kimono*."

"My, that sounds exciting!" Mimi said.

There was a knock on the door. It was Mitsuki. She was dressed in a light yellow *kimono*.

"You look pretty," Mimi said to the girl, motioning her to come in.

"I'm here to help Christina get dressed," Mitsuki said. "Christina will never tie the *obi* on tightly enough by herself. When I wear a *kimono*, my mother has to help me. I can't do it myself."

Christina had just bathed and put on a blouse and skirt. She didn't know where to begin when it came to putting on a *kimono*.

Mitsuki took charge, saying, "Just to be on the safe side, you can wear the clothes you have on. We'll just put the *kimono* on top of those." Giggling, Mitsuki added, "Then you won't have to worry if your belt comes undone. Also, it will be easier to play. If you wear *kimono* underwear, it's not so easy to run and jump."

First, Christina put on the white socks called *tabi* and put her feet into her new *geta*.

Then Mitsuki took the pink *kimono* off the hanger and held it up while Christina slid her arms into it. Christina pulled the front right side over the left, the way she always dressed.

"No, you can't do that," Mitsuki said with a frown. "That's how we dress dead people for burial. You must put the left side over the right side, like this," she added as she pulled the cloth across Christina's chest. "Now, hold it, while I wrap the belt." The *obi* was thick and very long.

Grant came in with his new camera just as Mitsuki began to tie the belt. He snapped pictures while Mitsuki ran around Christina, wrapping the belt tightly at her waist as she went.

"I feel like a silkworm in a cocoon!" Christina said as the belt tightened. She took a deep breath.

While Christina held the belt in place, Mitsuki wrapped two more narrow belts around her *obi*, one on top of the other, and tied those.

Stepping back, Mitsuki inspected Christina's new look. She said with pride in her work, "You are now ready for the cherry blossom festival. You look wonderful!"

Gazing in the mirror, Christina extended her arms as she slowly turned around. The sleeves flowed beautifully with her arm motions. The tightly bound robe and belt made her look tall and slim. She felt just like a Japanese princess!

Once Taro arrived, the four kids left for the festival, which Mitsuki called *sakura matsuri*. On the train, Mitsuki told her American guests about cherry blossom festivals.

"The cherry blossom is a favorite flower of the Japanese. To hold a cherry blossom festival means we are marking the start of spring, and new life. It makes everyone feel good to be alive. We are going to Ueno Park, which has more than 1,000 cherry trees. To see so many in bloom together is a wonder."

The kids arrived at Ueno Park, where row after row of trees were blooming with bright pink flowers.

Grant stood still, never having seen so much pink in his life. He ran underneath a tree and looked up. "It looks like a bunch of pink clouds overhead," he said, reaching for his camera.

The kids had brought a blanket and a picnic lunch. They picked a spot that was not too crowded with other people. Taro spread the blanket and Mitsuki set out the Japanese box lunches called *bento*. The *bento* boxes each contained a serving of cold rice with pieces of cooked fish and vegetables on the side.

The children munched their food as they watched people stroll through the park. Mitsuki pulled some *Craypas* crayons and paper out of a bag and began to draw. As Christina and the others watched, she first drew the beautiful scene of cherry blossom trees. Then she had Christina pose before her, and began to draw again.

Grant was amazed at Mitsuki's talent. "Christina," he said, "It looks just like you!"

When Mitsuki was done, she handed the portrait to Christina. "It's yours," she said. "To remember your stay in Japan."

Mitsuki then said to Grant, "You wanted to know how to write your name. I will show you how."

"Cool," Grant said. He sat down next to her.

Mitsuki said, "First you take the sounds in your name and match it to sounds in the Japanese alphabet. Your name is Grant. In Japanese, that would sound like Ga-ran-ta."

"That's the way your grandfather said my name at the airport," Grant said. "I like it— Ga-ran-ta!"

"Then you just take the characters for those sounds and put them together, like this."

Mitsuki took a piece of paper and a crayon. "Here are the characters for Ga, ran, and ta," she said. She wrote ガランタ. "Together, they make up your name, and that's how you would write your name."

Grant grabbed a crayon and copied the characters. Mitsuki then wrote the characters for Christina's name, クリチナ. The two American kids practiced writing their new Japanese names over and over and over.

Soon they heard drum music. Everyone picnicking near them stood up to watch an approaching parade.

"It's the dancers!" Mitsuki called out. "Let's go watch them."

About 30 women dressed in similar orange *kimono*s and carrying baskets sang a song as they danced. Each woman swung a big basket left to right as she danced. One of the women took Christina by the hand and drew her into the group of dancing women. Another woman handed Christina her basket. Soon Christina picked up the rhythm of the dance, and swung the basket left to right.

Taro and Mitsuki clapped as Grant took Christina's picture.

A fun day soon came to end, and it was time to go back to the hotel. Grant snapped pictures as the kids packed up their belongings and walked to the train station. He turned around to get a shot behind the other kids. He saw two giant men wearing men's *kimono*s trailing them. They wore angry scowls on their faces. A block later, the two men were still there!

Grant whispered to Christina, "Don't turn around, but I think there are two sumo players following us."

"Why do you say that?" Christina asked, eager to turn around and take a look. "And how do you know they are sumo players? Surely they aren't wearing loincloths!"

"It's their hairdos," Grant said. "Look, Sony. What do you think?"

Taro looked warily over his shoulder. He said, "Yes, they are sumo players. But why are they following us?"

"And why are they frowning at us?" Grant asked, getting a little worried.

Bad Times in the Japan Times

"Here it comes. The bullet train!" Grant yelled as he aimed his camera at the long, sleek train sliding up to the platform like a big snake.

"Why does the front of the train slope back?" Grant asked Taro, after snapping a few good shots.

"For the same reason airplanes have noses like that," Taro said. "Aerodynamics! The air easily moves around the train, letting it go faster."

"How fast will we go?" Grant asked. "Like a bullet?"

"Almost," Taro said. "When we get out of Tokyo the train will pick up speed, reaching about 270 kilometers per hour. That's 168 miles per hour."

"Cool. I can tell my friends back home I rode a bullet," Grant said, grabbing his backpack.

Like a shepherd leading his flock, Professor Kato helped his guests and grandchildren board the train and find good seats. Soon they were all very comfortably settled in, speeding on their way to Lake Hakone, a famous resort.

Grant set his camera on the window ledge to take pictures of the passing scenery. Taro read a Japanese electronics magazine while Mimi looked at the photos in a Japanese fashion magazine. Papa had his nose in the *Japan Times*, a popular English language newspaper. Mitsuki and Christina started a game of cards.

"I never saw a pack of cards look like these," Christina said, as Mitsuki pulled out a deck of cards decorated with different flower designs. "They are so pretty and so tiny."

"These are *hanafuda*, or flower cards," Mitsuki said. "There are forty-eight cards in a deck. The suits are made up of types of flowers, like cherry blossom, wisteria, or plum."

"How do you play them?" Christina asked, as she picked up the small cards and scanned through them, noting the design on each one.

"There are all sorts of games," Mitsuki said. "Some are just like the games you play. Let's play one like fish. Do you know how to play fish?"

Christina handed them back to Mitsuki and said, "Sure, I do!" Their game was on by the time the train was gaining speed.

"The buildings look like a blur," Grant said as the houses and stores outside the train flew by.

As they entered the countryside, the houses grew fewer in number and the train raced along open plains. Grant took pictures of traditional Japanese farm houses made of wood. There were rice fields with green rolling hills and mountains in the distance. One mountain stood apart larger and grander than all the rest, and seemed to grow in size as the train neared it. It was Mt. Fuji, now covered with white snow. Grant snapped away.

"It looks beautiful!" Mitsuki said with a beaming smile. "We Japanese are very proud of Mt. Fuji. It's a sacred mountain."

Christina looked around. There was a sudden silence in the train car. Most of the Japanese on the train had stopped what they were doing and stared at the mountain as if it were an angel descending from the heavens.

"We'll take a trip to see Mt. Fuji," Professor Kato promised.

Papa turned his eyes back to the newspaper. Something had caught his eye.

"Hey kids," he asked, "Weren't you at the sumo stable near the hotel the day before yesterday?

Christina said, "Yes, Papa, we were. That's when we got to shake hands with the sumo Grand Champion."

"Well, it says here that a sword was stolen from the trophy room that day. The sword belonged to the Grand Champion. It was given to him by the emperor."

"Oh my gosh!" Christina said. "Do you suppose that's why we heard police sirens near the stable? Maybe the sword was stolen about the time we were there!"

Papa read on, "The historic and valuable sword was lifted from its box and an imitation was put in its place. While the police have some suspects, the stable is offering a big reward for information leading to an arrest."

"Do you kids know anything?" Mimi asked. "It seems like mystery always follows you around, Christina."

"Well, I didn't see anything strange at the stable," Christina said, looking at Grant and not knowing how much she should say about the strange notes. She did not want to scare her grandmother. Those notes telling them to stay away from swords were probably just somebody's sick teasing.

"Looks like there's a mystery for you to solve, Christina," Mimi joked—*not knowing Christina was already deeply involved!*

Shakeups Galore

In no time, the bullet train pulled in to Atami. Professor Kato had rented a van to take everyone around Hakone and Mt. Fuji.

"Tonight, we sleep on *tatami*," Professor Kato said.

"Hurray!" Grant yelled as he jumped up and grabbed the back of the seat in front of him.

"Is the inn a real Japanese house? Like those," Grant asked, pointing to the tiny wooden houses lining the street.

"We are staying at a *ryokan*, a traditional Japanese inn," the professor replied. "And yes, it is very much like a Japanese house."

"Even the toilets?" Grant asked.

Professor Kato laughed. "Oh yes," he said, "even the toilets. They are fancy holes in the ground."

The van entered through a wooden gate, and followed a winding road up the side of a large hill. They drove to a spacious wooden house with a veranda and a curved tile roof.   It was built on the hillside, giving a lovely view of Lake Hakone in the distance. There were little gardens on two sides and a mountain brook running between the inn and the hill.

Professor Kato took them to their rooms down a narrow hallway.   On one side of the hallway, sliding doors opened to the garden and the brook. On the other side of the hallway, more sliding doors opened to their rooms.

"Awesome!" Grant said as he skipped into the kids' room. Straw *tatami* mats covered the floor, just as Professor Kato promised.   The only pieces of furniture were a small black floor lamp, and a low wooden table with four purple cushions set on the floor around it.

"Where do we sleep?" Grant asked.

Professor Kato slid open a closet door to reveal some thick cushions. He said, "When we get ready for bed, the maids will take these *futon*s out and spread them on the floor. You will sleep on them."

"Wow! This'll be more fun than camping out!" Grant said with glee.

"We will bathe in the hot springs later," Professor Kato said. "So, Taro-*kun* and Mitsuki-*chan*, why not explore the village with our guests?"

"Oh yes, let's go," Mitsuki urged her brother.

The kids charged out of the inn and jogged down the hill to the village. They passed a house that had a tall pole in front of it. From the pole hung three long banners shaped like fish. In the wind, the fish appeared to be jumping out of the water.

"Are those the Boys' Day banners?" Christina asked Mitsuki, remembering that Boys' Day was coming soon.

"Yes," Mitsuki answered. "Those are the carp streamers I was telling you about. We call them *koinobori*. You can see that there are three sons in that family."

"I should buy one," Christina said. "We can fly it at our house to show that we have one boy."

"Oh, Christina, that would be great!" Grant piped up. "I will love you forever."

"Yeah, yeah," Christina teased Grant as she went into a toy store. "Someday, when you are

being a pain, I'll remind you of those words."
She bought a large green carp banner. Mitsuki
arranged to have the carp delivered to the inn.

The kids still had places to see before going
back. They popped into a variety of little shops
selling souvenirs, tofu, fish, and local vegetables.
They raced up the hill to the mountain brook,
and splashed their hands in the cold water.

When the kids returned to the hotel, it was
time to bathe in the hot springs. They all
changed into the light summer *kimono*s hanging
in their closets.

"Don't we need swim suits?" Grant asked.

"Oh no," Papa said. "We are going to wear our
birthday suits."

"Birthday suits? Do I have one of those,
Mimi? I don't remember packing it," Grant
asked, very worried.

"We're going naked," Christina said,
matter-of-factly.

"Nekkid?" Grant howled. "I am not going
nekkid with Christina in a hot spring!"

Papa laughed. "You don't have to," he said.
"We guys are going to one hot spring and the
girls are going to another one."

"Thank goodness," Grant sighed. "In that
case, let's go!"

The hot springs were steamy and relaxing, like a large swimming pool filled with hot water. Men and boys swam and lounged in the deep end. In the shallow end, boys splashed each other in water fights.

At first, Grant was a little shy, holding a washcloth in front of him as he made his way to the pool. But as soon as he jumped in, he had a great time, splashing Taro and Papa with the warm water. Professor Kato looked very much at home, leaning back against the side of the pool, up to his chin in water, with a towel tied around his head.

Afterward, everyone gathered back at the inn in one of the guestrooms to eat a Japanese meal. They sat on cushions on the floor. Maids served tea in little cups. Everyone enjoyed rice and vegetables from round bowls.

After the meal, the hotel maids arranged the *futon*s on the floor. Papa announced it was time for bed. "No staying up all night talking," he said. "We have to get up early."

The kids crawled into their *futon*s. Mitsuki turned off the lamp.

"These are just like sleeping bags," Grant whispered to Christina.

"It's not as hard as sleeping on the ground," Christina whispered back. She snuggled under the heavy covers and began to doze off. Suddenly, the floor began to shake. A vase toppled off the table and crashed to the floor.

From the next room someone yelled "*Jishen!*"

"Earthquake!" Taro yelled as he jumped up. "Everybody get up. Run outside! The building could fall down."

Grant and Christina, still in their *kimono*s, jumped up and bolted out the door on the heels of Taro and Mitsuki. Outside, they joined Mimi, Papa, and Professor Kato, who looked like he just woke up. His usually very neat hair and mustache were rumpled.

Professor Kato apologized for the inconvenience. He added, "When the ground shakes badly, it's best to leave the building. We do it all the time because earthquakes are so common in Japan, and often quite deadly."

It seemed like hours before the innkeeper told everyone it was safe to go back to bed.

"After that excitement," Mimi said, "I don't know who could go back to sleep."

The kids went to their room, but they didn't feel like sleeping. Grant spotted the carp banner

Christina had bought for him. It had been delivered to the room and was neatly folded. "Sony, let's see it," Grant said as he grabbed one end. Taro grabbed the other. As the two boys stretched it out full length, a note fell out. All the kids froze. They looked at each other, not knowing what to say.

Christina slowly reached for the note. She read:

Fishing for swords will get you into trouble!

"What does that mean?" Taro said. "Whoever is writing these notes has a thing about swords!"

Christina said, "Earthquakes and now another weird note. It seems like there's lots of things to worry about in Japan." *She didn't get much sleep that night. And it wasn't because the futon was harder than a mattress!*

Fits of Mt. Fuji

The next morning, Papa got the kids up early. It was time to see the sights of Hakone. With Professor Kato at the wheel, the group drove around Lake Ashi, a clear blue mountain lake formed from the crater of an old volcano. The lake was surrounded by pine trees and hills. The image of snow-covered Mt. Fuji reflected upside down in the water.

Professor Kato pointed at the lake and said, "It is very peaceful now, but once it was a large hole, spewing fire and ash everywhere. It is one of many old volcanoes in Japan. Most of the volcanoes are sleeping but about 60 are very active."

"Active—what does that mean?" Grant asked, somewhat confused. "And how exactly does a volcano sleep?"

"A sleeping volcano means that the volcano has not shot up gas and lava in a very long time. But it could still do so at anytime. Mt. Fuji is a sleeping volcano."

"And when a volcano wakes up, it gets nasty?" Grant asked. "Like a mean giant?"

"Like a mean giant with an **acute** stomach ache!" Professor Kato said. "You better take off when one starts belching!"

"And I used to like to hear a good burp!" Grant said as he eyed Mt. Fuji in the distance. "I hope Mt. Fuji is sleeping soundly."

Professor Kato said, "Japan is made up of a lot of sleeping volcanic giants and some waking ones. That makes Japan part of the Ring of Fire, a series of hot spots around the Pacific Ocean where many earthquakes and volcanoes shake up the world."

"That earthquake we had last night—does that mean a volcano is going to erupt?" Christina asked. "It shook things up."

Papa added, "I heard on the U.S. Armed Forces radio station this morning that the earthquake was a 6.0 on the Richter scale. That is pretty strong."

Professor Kato said, "It was bad. It scared me. I hope it doesn't mean a volcano is getting ready to erupt."

"Maybe the giants are just having bad dreams," Grant guessed. Maybe they're tossing and turning and making the ground shake."

"Speaking of volcanoes, shall we take a trip to Mt. Fuji now?" Professor Kato asked.

Everyone agreed to get a closer look at the sleeping giant.

"Can we all of us climb Mt. Fuji?" Christina asked, hopefully.

"*Sumimasen.* No, not now," Professor Kato said. "The top of Mt. Fuji is now too cold with very dangerous winds and snow. In the summer after the snow melts, people can climb safely. I climbed it once when I was young like you. I couldn't do it now."

Christina and Grant were a little disappointed but they were too polite to say so. Grant said, "Will we get close enough to hear the giant snore?"

Professor Kato laughed and said, "That might happen."

They drove for a while between large hills that soon became mountains. Mt. Fuji got bigger and bigger. They ate at a restaurant with the beautiful giant looming in the big picture window above their table. After lunch, they got in the car and headed to the southeast part of the mountain.

"I heard there was a little bit of volcanic activity happening here," Professor Kato said. "Sometimes, if it is safe, the police let tourists come and take pictures. Let's see if we can see something interesting."

As the van climbed up the side of the mountain, a stream of traffic began to flow from the opposite direction, passing them in the other lane.

"This is strange," Professor Kato said, "we are the only ones going in this direction."

"What do they know that we don't?" Mimi asked, peering out the window.

The van turned a corner and everyone had a clear view of the road ahead. The police had set up a road block. When the van reached the road block, a police officer waved his hand, telling Professor Kato to turn around.

Professor Kato asked the policeman some questions in Japanese and then turned to his guests. He said, "We have to go back. A fissure on Mt. Fuji is erupting!"

At that moment, they heard a roar. Over another hill ahead, they saw a jet of white steam shoot high up in the air.

"Mt. Fuji must have a bad tummy ache," Grant cried. "It's starting to throw up. We better get out of here."

When Professor Kato dropped off his guests at their Tokyo hotel, the adults and kids went to their rooms to relax after the adventurous trip.

Christina and Grant had settled in their beds when someone knocked on the door. Christina opened the door to see a hotel bellboy holding a box.

"Someone left a present for you, Miss," he said as he gave Christina the gift. She thanked the bellboy and closed the door. Christina looked Grant and said, "Who would give me a gift?"

"Open it, open it," Grant cried, excited by a present. "Maybe it's from Mitsuki."

Christina took off the wrapping paper. It was a *kokeshi* doll, a hand-carved wooden figure of a girl in a *kimono*. Its head was round and its body was long like a wooden tube. Christina slowly took the head off the doll's body. She was shocked to see a note inside the tube.

"Not another note!" Christina wailed.

"What does it say?" Grant asked, alarmed.

Christina read:

新宿区歌舞伎町 30-10

**You kids!
Your
fingerprints
are on the
sword!**

She looked at her brother and said, "Our fingerprints are on the sword—what sword? What does that mean?"

"The sword stolen at the sumo stable?" Grant asked, remembering what Papa had read in the newspaper.

"I never touched that sword!" Christina cried.

"Neither did I!" Grant said.

Mulling the Pieces of the Puzzle

The next day, Taro and Mitsuki took Christina and Grant to see a Japanese puppet show. It was different from any the American kids had seen before. Mitsuki explained that Japanese puppet shows date from the 16th century and were the most popular form of entertainment in Japan before movies and television.

"The stage looks like it is set for a *kabuki* play," Christina said, "with gold silk screens in the background, and a big wooden bridge in the foreground."

"Maybe it's because some *kabuki* plays were once written for puppets instead of actors," Mitsuki said.

On the right side of the stage, a musician strummed on a Japanese three-stringed guitar. Another man chanted the story of the puppet play in Japanese. Finally, three people, completely covered in black cloth from head to toe, appeared on stage.

"Why are they dressed like that?" Grant whispered. "Are they ghosts?"

"No," Mitsuki said quietly. "Dressing in black makes it easy to pretend they are not there—like the *ninja*. The men in black will handle the puppets."

Sure enough, the three men moved behind a table covered with a dark cloth. They lifted up a large puppet dressed as a Japanese *samurai*. The puppet jumped to life as its arms swung a sword outward toward the audience.

"It's huge! It must be almost four feet tall," Christina whispered to Mitsuki. "No wonder it takes three people to move one puppet."

Mitsuki said in a low voice, "One man controls the head and right arm, another moves the left arm, and the third moves the feet."

The kids were dazzled as more large puppets came to life through the work of the "invisible" handlers. There were puppets of all kinds: a geisha dancer with a white painted face in a shimmering red *kimono*, a ghost that dreamily floated through the air, and a clown that hopped around the stage.

Near the end of the show, Mitsuki noticed Christina's pinched eyebrows and rumpled smile. "Is there something wrong?" she asked her friend.

Christina said, "I feel like one of those puppets. Someone's trying to pull me here and there. I'll tell you after the show. We got another note last night."

"Oh, no," Mitsuki cried.

After the puppet show, the kids walked back to the hotel by taking a winding path through a large Japanese garden. The garden was filled with bamboo groves and small pine trees. Here and there a small fish pond appeared to delight visitors. The kids found a wooden bench next to a stone lantern and sat down. Christina told their hosts about the note from the night before.

"Not another note," Taro said. "This is really getting scary. And you say this last note accuses you and Grant of taking a sword?"

"We didn't take any swords, you know that," Grant said firmly.

"Of course," Mitsuki said, sighing.

"In fact, we lost a sword," Christina said. "Isn't that strange? I was thinking about what you said the night of the earthquake when we got that note wrapped in the fish banner. You said the person sending these notes must have 'a thing about swords.' I think that's true. It has to be somebody with a crazy interest in swords or knows we bought a sword, like the old man with the bike or the man we saw at the airport."

"The guy we also saw at the hotel stealing the tip money?" Grant asked. "He did tell you to stay out of his way when he gave you that dirty look."

"That guy had slick, sticky fingers. He could've easily stolen the sword," Christina said. "But I didn't see him at the sumo stable. Did you?"

"No," everyone said together as they looked at each other.

Christina then asked, "Why are we getting these notes? And why was Papa's sword stolen? None of it makes sense."

"If anybody can figure out how the pieces fit, it's you," Taro said to make Christina feel better.

Christina continued thinking out loud, attempting to put the pieces together. "There is another strange thing—those sumo players that followed us from the Cherry Blossom Festival. Why were they following us? Did they also think we stole the sword from the sumo stable?"

"Yeah," Taro agreed. "Why would sumo players care about a bunch of kids?"

Christina pulled a piece of paper from her pocket. It was the note she found in the *kokeshi* doll the night before. She unfolded it.

"I was looking at the note and didn't notice the paper it was written on," Christina remarked. "Looking at it now, I think there's a clue for us." She held the note out for the other kids to read. "See that Japanese writing? I remember seeing those Japanese characters on a street sign in Tokyo."

"You are right, Christina, that's a Shinjuku address," Taro said. "You have a good memory. And that's smart thinking."

"What if we go to this address and see if we can find some more clues about who's sending the notes?" Christina asked.

"We should do it tomorrow. Look, it's already getting dark," Mitsuki said as she gazed at the gloomy shade hiding the garden pathway. Christina shivered as a cold breeze blew against her neck.

More Than a Walk in the Park!

Their talk about mysteries done, the kids chattered about what they wanted to eat for dinner. Suddenly, in the dimming light, they saw two big, shadowy figures coming at them, blocking their way on the path.

Taro said, "I don't like the way they look. Let's run." Taro took off in the other direction, with Mitsuki, Christina, and Grant on his heels.

Grant yelled, "They're following us! It's those sumo men. I can tell by their hairdos!"

"Run faster," Taro yelled.

"I can't, Taro," Grant wailed with a **forlorn** look on his face. "My shoe is coming undone!"

Taro, Christina and Mitsuki turned back to stay with Grant. They couldn't abandon him to two angry sumo players.

The large men were soon upon them, and had the kids surrounded, blocking any front and rear escapes. The scared kids huddled together in a circle. The taller man fired questions at Taro in Japanese.

"What do they want?" Christina whispered to Mitsuki, whose knees were shaking.

"They...they...want to know who stole the Grand Champion's sword," Mitsuki stammered.

One of the sumo players pulled out a picture of a short sword from inside his *kimono* and asked if it belonged to one of the kids. The kids gathered around to look.

"That looks like our missing sword," Grant cried. "I lost it in the crowd!"

"Maybe the thief took your sword in the crowd," Christina said, "to make it look like someone else did it."

Taro repeated Christina's words in Japanese for the sumo players to hear.

"The sumo player says the thief replaced the historic sword he stole with this one in the picture," Taro said. "And a grainy video tape recorded the act. The person stealing the sword was not Japanese and had brown hair. From the rear, the thief looked like you, Christina. The hair looked the same."

"I should never have gotten my hair cut so short!" Christina said, as she stamped her foot. "And tell them I didn't steal it. And neither did Grant."

Taro explained all this to the sumo players, who said they wanted to talk to the kids' parents. Taro explained that Professor Kato, Mimi, and Papa were in charge of the kids. He offered to take the sumo players back to the hotel to talk to the adults.

At the hotel, Christina told the whole story from the beginning, including the notes. She said she didn't feel like she had to tell Mimi or Papa because the earlier messages just warned the kids to stay away from swords. Those were just weird notes, nothing more.

Mimi said, "Well, Christina, it looks like you managed to land yourself a mystery!"

And Papa added, "I bet you already know how to solve it, young lady."

"I don't know who took Papa's sword or the Grand Champion's sword," Christina said. "But we do have a clue about who's sending us notes about swords. It's on this paper written in Japanese." She offered the note with the address to the sumo players.

The biggest sumo player wrote down the address. He said they would contact the police. The other sumo player, in a very grave voice, said *"Sumimasen"* to Professor Kato, and then something else the Americans didn't understand. Professor Kato laughed out loud.

"What's so funny, Professor Kato?" Christina asked.

Professor Kato said, "The sumo player thinks *Garanta-kun* has an honest face. He doesn't think the boy stole the sword, and he can't imagine why you would. But he isn't entirely sure yet. In any case, the sumo stable needs to keep your sword as evidence. When the real thief is caught it will be returned to you."

Winning the Prize in the Pachinko Parlor!

"We can't have anyone thinking Christina and Grant took the sword," Taro told his sister. "We must help them find this address."

"But what if we run into some bad guys?" Mitsuki asked.

"How will the bad guys know us? We are just some average Japanese," Taro joked. "We don't stand out in a crowd like Christina and Grant. We must help them. We helped them get into this mess."

The next day, all four kids set out to find the address written on the note. After walking down a few back streets in Shinjuku, they tracked down the address. "Look!" cried Mitsuki. "It's a *pachinko* parlor."

"What's that?" Christina asked.

Taro said, "It's a place where adults can play games like pinball. It's not really gambling because gambling is not allowed in Japan. It's more like your amusement park contests where you pay money to throw balls at some bottles. If you knock down the bottles, you get a small prize. In *pachinko*, you can turn the balls you win into money at one of these shops near the *pachinko* parlor." Taro pointed to some small convenience stores lining the street. These shops also sold snacks, soft drinks and newspapers.

"It really looks smoky and dark inside," Christina said, trying to get a peek through the window.

"It's not a place for kids," Taro said. "We better stay outside."

Christina said, "Let's wait a while and see what happens."

Taro went to one of the shops and bought some rice crackers called *sembei*. He passed the crackers around for the kids to munch on while they waited. They sat down on the curb and tried to ignore the stares of the people passing by.

Christina soon got bored and tried once again to peer into the window of the *pachinko* parlor. Suddenly, among the Japanese playing the pinball machines, she noticed a brown-haired man wearing a black leather jacket with the characters for Japan—*Nihon*—written on the back.

"Taro, Mitsuki, Grant, come and look!" Christina hissed. "Oh my gosh, I think it's the guy at the airport. He's playing *pachinko*. Did he steal the sword?"

All the kids pressed their noses against the window to look for the man Christina had identified.

Taro said to Christina, "In the dim light, that guy in the black jacket does look a little like you from the rear."

"Thanks a lot," Christina said, fuming.

Suddenly, the man started jumping up and down.

"I think he's won some balls," Taro said, trying to get a better view through the window.

The man neatly scooped up the steel balls he won and thrust them in a bag. He turned around. The kids got a good look at his face. *There was no doubt it was the same man who was at the airport—and who stole the tip money in the hotel. Had Christina tracked down the culprit?*

Shock and Awe

"That slick character who stole the tip money at the hotel," Taro said as he tried to get a better look of the man through the window in the *pachinko* parlor. "He's definitely capable of lifting the sword without anybody noticing."

"Mr. Slicky himself," Grant agreed, saying the words slowly. "Because he is slick, with sticky fingers."

"But if he did it," Christina asked, "How can we prove it? And how can we prove he actually sent us the notes?"

"That will be hard to do," Mitsuki said.

The man Grant called Mr. Slicky suddenly headed to the entrance of the *pachinko* parlor. The kids nearly stumbled over themselves in moving away from the building entrance. But it was too late. Mr. Slicky saw them.

He looked at Christina and sneered, "How did you follow me here? I warned you..."

Christina decided to take a chance. "Why were you writing us those scary notes?" she asked boldly. "We don't need to be warned to stay away from swords. We're not little kids!"

As the man pushed his way past the kids he only said, "I hope they scared you! You should be scared."

Christina would not let him talk down to her. She said, "Did you take our sword?"

Mr. Slicky spun around, his mouth a big "O." He bolted down the street, not seeing a man on a bicycle rounding the corner. The bicycle ran smack into Mr. Slicky. Both men sprawled onto the cement. Mr. Slicky's bag of balls burst, bouncing and rolling all over the place. Everyone on the street stopped to stare. Taro ran to help the man who fell off the bicycle. Grant took out his camera and began taking pictures of Mr. Slicky.

"You bratty kid," Mr. Slicky snarled, as he bent over to scoop up the balls. Then as he leaned far forward, a long thin object fell out of his jacket, clattering to the ground.

"The Grand Champion's sword!" Grant cried as he saw the sword separate from its case and slide among the rolling balls.

Grant hurriedly snapped more pictures of Mr. Slicky trying to grab the sword. He yelled, "I'm going to show these pictures to the sumo players!"

At that moment, two policemen and the two sumo players from the night before charged out of a convenience store next door. They surrounded Mr. Slicky. After taking the sword from him, one of the policemen put Mr. Slicky in handcuffs and took him away to a waiting police car.

The other policeman said to Taro in Japanese, "We were watching this *pachinko* parlor all morning because we had the address your American friends gave the sumo players. Tell them they have been very helpful in more ways than one! They not only led us to this place, but the young man here helped us trick the thief into showing us he had the sword!"

Taro told the kids in English what the policeman said. Mitsuki said to Christina as she patted her on the back, "It looks like you solved another mystery!"

The policeman shook the kids' hands. The sumo players came over and gave the kids a bow, which the kids returned, remembering to bow more deeply.

"*Arigato, arigato,*" the sumo players kept saying over and over. "Thank you. Thank you. We will be happy to tell the sumo stable manager and the Grand Champion about this. The Grand Champion will be very pleased."

A Banner Day

Back at the hotel, the kids told Professor Kato, Mimi, and Papa what happened.

Taro said, "If Christina hadn't noticed those Japanese characters were a street address, we would never have solved this mystery."

Christina added, "Well, Grant was fast thinking to take those pictures. It made the thief so upset he dropped the sword for everyone to see."

"It was lucky for all of you the police were already on the scene waiting to see what the suspect would do," Papa said with a serious voice. "They were able to catch him and you weren't hurt."

"Don't worry, Papa," Christina said, "I didn't think he would have done anything to hurt us. He was just a thief."

"Well, let's celebrate," Papa said. "Mimi's talk with the mystery writers' association went well. And you both solved a real mystery. I think we should all have a good time." Papa paused and then asked Professor Kato, "Where could we go to celebrate, kids and adults— everybody together?"

Papa was interrupted by a knock on the door.

Mimi opened the door to see the two sumo players. They had big smiles on their faces.

Professor Kato invited them in. He spoke for a while with the two men in Japanese. Then he turned to his American guests and said, "I think we have the answer on how to celebrate. These sumo wrestlers say that the Grand Champion himself wants to thank everyone for helping to solve this crime. He is inviting all of us to Tokyo Disneyland. Would you like to go?"

"Disneyland? Japan has a Disneyland?" Grant asked, not believing his ears. "Oh please, Mimi, Papa, can we go?"

From the big grins on everyone's faces, Mimi and Papa could see that Disneyland would be a perfect place to celebrate.

The next day, a long black limousine pulled up in front of the hotel. People in the lobby stared when they recognized the sumo Grand Champion getting out of the car. He invited his waiting guests to climb into the limousine. Grant got to sit next to the Grand Champion. With Taro's help as a translator, they talked about sumo all the way to Disneyland.

There was a pleasant surprise at Disneyland. As special guests of an important person, the kids did not have to wait in the long lines to hop aboard the rides.

"I sure like this VIP treatment," smiled Taro. "Christina, I am pleased to be friends with a famous mystery-solver!"

Christina smiled from ear to ear.

"Can we ride some more?" Grant asked, enjoying every minute of his day at Tokyo Disneyland. "This is the best day ever!"

The adults were getting a little dizzy and tired from all the rides and excitement. The Grand Champion said, "Aren't you hungry? Why don't we get something to eat?"

"Are we eating raw fish?" Grant asked, secretly hoping they weren't.

"No," said the sumo player. "How about an American hamburger?"

"A real American hamburger?" Grant yelled as he jumped for joy.

"About as real as you can get in Japan," Taro said, laughing.

The Grand Champion said, "Come this way." He led all his guests to another section of Disneyland where the buildings looked just like they do in the old American cowboy movies. "This is Westernland. We are going to the Hungry Bear Restaurant. We made reservations there."

"I am hungry as a bear," Grant said. "Having a good time makes me hungry."

They arrived at the restaurant and were led to a table reserved for them. The kids giggled as they ordered their favorite American dishes.

As Grant stuffed his mouth with his juicy hamburger, he felt someone tap him on the shoulder. It was Mickey Mouse!

Grant was stunned. He could not believe his eyes.

Mimi laughed and said, "For once, it looks like Grant has nothing to say."

Mickey shook Grant's hand with his big white glove. Grant managed to say, "Hi, I mean *Konnichi wa*." Then Grant asked Mickey, "Do you speak English here or Japanese?"

Mickey said he spoke both, but Christina detected a slight American accent in his voice. Then Mickey shook Christina's hand.

"Can we get a picture with you?" Christina asked. Mickey nodded and the kids gathered around him before he left to visit with other Disneyland guests.

After the meal, the Grand Champion again thanked Christina and Grant for their help in returning his sword. He explained that the sword was very special to him since it was a gift from the emperor. Then he said, "I have something for you." He handed a beautiful blue box to Christina. She opened it to see a banner with the Grand Champion's name written on it. He had also autographed it. Then he took out another box and handed it to Grant. "I think this belongs to you," the Grand Champion said.

"The sword for Papa?" Grant asked, as he opened the box. "Yesssss!" he shouted, pumping his fist in the air. "After Tokyo Disneyland, and now this, my visit to Japan is complete! *Konnichi wa, konnichi wa, konnichi wa!*"

About the Author

Carole Marsh is an author and publisher who has written many works of fiction and non-fiction for young readers. She travels throughout the United States and around the world to research her books. In 1979, Carole Marsh was named Communicator of the Year for her corporate communications work with major national and international corporations.

Marsh is the founder and CEO of Gallopade International, established in 1979. Today, Gallopade International is widely recognized as a leading source of educational materials for every state and many countries. Marsh and Gallopade were recipients of the 2004 Teachers' Choice Award. Marsh has written more than 50 Carole Marsh Mysteries™. In 2007, she was named Georgia Author of the Year. Years ago, her children Michele and Michael were the original characters in her mystery books. Today, they continue the Carole Marsh Books tradition by working at Gallopade. By adding grandchildren Grant and Christina as new mystery characters, she has continued the tradition for a third generation.

Ms. Marsh welcomes correspondence from her readers. You can e-mail her at fanclub@gallopade.com, visit carolemarshmysteries.com, or write to her in care of Gallopade International, P.O. Box 2779, Peachtree City, Georgia, 30269 USA.

Built-In Book Club

Talk About It!

1. Does Japan seem like an exotic country to you? What country or countries might seem "exotic" to Japanese children?

2. Why is Christina so interested in Japanese culture?

3. After reading this book, would you say that Japanese kids are like American kids in a lot of ways? What are some ways they are similar, and what are some ways they are different?

4. Why do you think a samurai sword is a very strong symbol in Japanese culture?

5. Sumo players are very popular in Japan. Can you think of some American athletes who get the same kind of admiration and attention?

6. Do you find the Japanese alphabet interesting? Do you think it would be hard to learn? Why or why not?

7. Do you know why Japan has so many earthquakes?

8. The children were offered some different types of food in Japan, like a lunch of cold rice, fish, and vegetables. Are you willing to try new foods when you visit new places?

9. What did you learn about Japan that you did not know before?

10. Would you like to visit Japan? If so, what would you like to see and do there?

Built-In Book Club

Bring it to Life!

1. Using the *Katakana* Alphabet in the back of the book, write your name in *Katakana*. First, find similar sounds in *Katakana* that closely match the sounds in your name. Then find the *Katakana* character that goes with the sound. Write the characters down. You can draw these on card stock, color them, cut them out, and string them on black cord to wear around your neck.

2. Make *origami* paper toys. Just about any kind of paper of any size can be used as long as it is easy to fold. *Origami* paper can often be purchased toy or craft stores. Search the Internet fo find websites with instructions on how to fold the paper and make some cool items!

3. Make a *koinobori* banner from either paper or cloth. Take a long rectangular piece of plain paper or cloth and fold it lengthwise. Sew, glue, or tape the side. Paint a big round eye and some scales on the *koinobori* like in the image at the upper right. Add some fun streamers. It can be hung from a pole in front of the house on May 5th or any day you want to have some fun!

4. Try making your own Japanese clothes. Get a bathrobe—the bigger the better—and then get a long wide scarf and wrap it around you. You may need a friend to help you. Make sure the bathrobe and belt fit closely to the body. Hold a fan. Put on some flip-flops and try walking around holding the fan. How do you feel? (Very comfortable, probably!)

5. Try using chopsticks. Follow the instructions that Taro gives Grant in the book. If you don't have a pair of chopsticks, you can practice by using two pencils or sticks, but don't put them in your mouth. The next time you go to a Chinese or Japanese restaurant, ask for a pair of chopsticks and test your new skill!

Glossary

 acute: very strong and deep (acute pain); or very sensitive (acute hearing)

Arigato: "Thank you."

callous: emotionally hard; unfeeling

chan: used after a little girl's name, like "Little Miss"

divine: of or like God or a god

emulate: imitate; try to equal or match something

forlorn: lonely and sad; unhappy

futon: sleep bedding like a large cushion that is stored away at night

geta: wooden shoes with a strap between the toes. They are usually elevated by two wood pieces running cross-wise under the soles to keep the wearer's foot dry on muddy streets.

hanafuda: a deck of Japanese cards with designs of flowers and plants for the suits instead of hearts, clubs or spades. The cards are usually small, about one inch by two inches in size.

hara-kiri: a ritual whereby a *samurai* killed himself to keep his honor. The words mean "to cut the bowel," indicating that the samurai cut across his stomach to perform the deed.

jishen: an earthquake

kabuki: traditional Japanese folk theatre

Kanji: Chinese characters in the Japanese language. Japanese uses several thousand characters in daily use to form part of the writing system. It is a major challenge for Japanese children to learn the commonly used ones, and takes years of study to master reading and writing them.

kimono: a long robe with long sleeves. Both men and women wear *kimono*; the differences for men and ladies are in the colors and designs.

koinobori: a brightly colored cloth banner in the shape of a fish flown in front of a house on Boys' Day, May 5. Flying a *koinobori* tells everyone that a boy lives in the house. If there are three boys in a family, the house will fly three *koinobori*.

Konnichi wa: "How are you?"

kun: used after a little boy's name, like "Little Mister"

Katakana: the Japanese alphabet used for foreign words

kokeshi: a type of doll made of two wooden pieces. The head sits on top of the separate tube-like body. The doll's hair, face, hands, feet, and clothing are usually painted on by an artist.

Nihon: the Japanese word for Japan

ninja: a spy or assassin in old Japan. *Ninjas* are famous for wearing black clothing and scarves to hide their appearance in the night.

obi: a wide belt that is tied around a *kimono*

origami: brightly colored paper folded into a variety of shapes

oshiburi: a small wet washcloth given to guests in restaurants to clean their hands and faces before a meal

pachinko: a game like pinball where the player tries to win more balls by feeding balls into a machine

rashu owa: rush hour. Tokyo's huge population makes coming and going to work a real challenge for traffic, train riders and people walking on the streets.

ryokan: a traditional Japanese inn with *tatami* on the floor and often a garden on the grounds

samurai: a warrior of old Japan. The *samurai* served a lord, much like the knights in feudal Europe.

san: used after adults' names for both men and women

sembei: a rice cracker commonly eaten like potato chips. Sometimes seaweed is wrapped around it.

Sumimasen: "I am sorry."

tabi: socks with a slit between the big and next toe. *Tabi* are worn with *geta*.

tatami: straw mats that cover a floor of a Japanese house. The size of a traditional Japanese room was measured in the number of *tatami* in it.

teriyaki: meat broiled with soy sauce. In America, it has come to mean the name of the sauce on the meat.

yen: Japanese money, the equivalent to "dollar."

Katakana:

The Japanese Alphabet for Use
with Non-Japanese Words

ア a	イ i	ウ u	エ e	オ o
バ ba	ビ bi	ブ bu	ベ be	ボ bo
ビャ bya		ビュ byu		ビョ byo
ダ da	ヂ ji	ツ zu	デ de	ド do
チャ cha		チュ chu	チェ che	チョ cho
ガ ga	ギ gi	グ gu	ゲ ge	ゴ go
ギャ gya		ギュ gyu		ギョ gyo
ハ ha	ヒ hi	フ hu	ヘ he	ホ ho
ヒャ hya		ヒュ hyu		ヒョ hyo
ジャ ja		ジュ ju	ジェ je	ジョ jo
カ ka	キ ki	ク ku	ケ ke	コ ko
キャ kya		キュ kyu		キョ kyo
マ ma	ミ mi	ム mu	メ me	モ mo

Note: Each Japanese character appears above
its letter or sound.

ミヤ mya		ミュ myu		ミヨ myo
ナ na	ニ ni	ヌ nu	ネ ne	ノ no
ニヤ nya		ニュ nyu		ニヨ nyo
バ pa	ピ pi	プ pu	ペ pe	ポ po
バヤ pya		バユ pyu		バヨ pyo
ラ ra	リ ri	ル ru	レ re	ロ ro
リヤ rya		リュ ryu		リヨ ryo
サ sa	シ shi	ス su	セ se	ソ so
シヤ sha		シュ shu	シェ she	ショ sho
タ ta	チ ti (chi)	ツ tsu	テ te	ト to
ヤ ya		ユ yu		ヨ yo
ザ za	ジ zi	ズ zu	ゼ ze	ゾ zo
ワ wa	ン n			

Enjoy this exciting excerpt from

The Mystery on the

Great Wall of China

1 A Slow Boat to China

"Mimi," Christina asked, "are you going to write a mystery set in China?"

Christina's grandmother just continued to stare out the Air China airplane window with a dreamy look in her eyes.

"Mimi?" Christina repeated. "Mimi?"

"Oh, I heard you," Mimi finally answered. "How can I?" she asked her granddaughter. "China is so...so...well, just look!"

The four heads of Mimi, Papa, Christina, and Grant huddled together to stare out at the enormous mountain range far beneath them. Traversing the hillsides was a long—indeed, endless, or at least as far as they could see in either direction—stone snake.

"The Great Wall of China," Papa intoned in his deep, cowboy voice.

"*Great* seems like a small word for it," Mimi agreed breathlessly.

Christina shook her head sadly. "We'll never get to see all of China, will we?"

"Not in all our lifetimes put together," admitted Mimi.

Grant pressed his nose against the glass. "Well, can we at least walk the Great Wall?" he asked hopefully.

Papa laughed. "Just part of it, or all the *thousands* of miles of it?"

Christina and Grant gasped together. They knew that China was one of the largest and most mysterious and exotic countries in the world. They'd heard Mimi talk about its history of emperors and dynasties and culture. Papa said that with its billions of people, it was an important trade partner with the United States and other countries.

"Mimi," Christina said, "I think you're right— you probably can't write a mystery big enough to get all of China in it."

"What?" squealed Grant. "But I already told our pen pals Li and Cong that you would. In fact," he added, blushing, "I, uh, I told them that they could be characters in the book."

"Grant!" scolded Christina. "You know Mimi only picks kids who go to her fan club website and apply to be a character."

"But they did!" Grant argued. "A long time ago, back when we first started writing postcards to each other."

"Oh, that's right," said Christina. "I remember now. Li said she would be a good character because she was cute and sweet and smart in school and loves to read mysteries in Chinese *and* English."

"And Cong said he was good at figuring out clues, and he knows martial arts, and he likes to break rules," Grant added.

"Just what we need," grumbled Papa, "more little rule breakers." He pointed to Christina and Grant and grinned. "And why do you two varmints think you make such good mystery book characters?"

Now Grant and Christina grinned. "Because we're your grandkids, of course!"

Christina tugged at Mimi's sleeve. "So will you write a mystery about China, please?"

Mimi just continued to stare out the window at the magnificent landscape below. "Sure," she finally agreed in a dreamy voice. "Just get me off this airplane and put me on a slow boat to China...and I'll be done in a few hundred years."

When the red lights flashed FASTEN SEATBELTS in preparation for landing, Grant and Christina hopped back across the aisle into their own seats.

"Christina," Grant whispered. "We can't wait that long for a new book—we'll be old and gray. We've got to help Mimi."

"How?" Christina asked, shaking her head.

Grant stared out the window. "By helping her find a mystery—real quick. REAL QUICK!"

"Grant," Christina said, "I don't think you find a mystery, I think *it* finds *you*."

Grant looked back out the window as China rushed up at them as they began their descent. *Oh, no,* he thought to himself. *I will find Mimi a mystery. I can find Mimi a mystery. China is so mysterious that I'll bet I find a mystery even before we even get off...*

Suddenly, Grant spied something peculiar in the seatback pocket. While his sister filled out her immigration papers and admired her passport picture one more time, he gently pulled a ragged piece of old parchment paper out of the pocket. When he looked closely at it, he grinned. It was a treasure map, complete with plenty of directions, an X to mark the spot where the treasure could be found, and even a skull and crossbones warning. Or was that a dragon?

Quickly, Grant folded the map and tucked it his pocket. He smiled a little secret smile. *Wait until Christina, Li, and Cong see this! Of course, it is all in Chinese, but that will make the mystery even more fun to solve—won't it?*

Confucius Say...

Papa had been pretty disappointed that he hadn't been able to fly the *Mystery Girl,* his little red and white airplane, into China. That's how they usually traveled around, or either on Papa's green and white boat, also named *Mystery Girl.* But rules were rules and China seemed to have lots and lots of rules.

"Boy, are we ever going to get out of this airport?" grumbled Mimi. They had been through passport lines, immigration lines, and bathroom lines. Mimi was not fond of lines.

As they stood in line, Grant kept peeking at the map in his pocket. He was curious about the golden dragon with jade green curlicues all around it.

"What are you looking at?" Christina startled him by saying.

"Oh, nothing," said Grant, secretively. He just smiled and stuffed the map back in his pocket. He heard the dry parchment crinkle and hoped he hadn't torn the map.

"Confucius say...he who watches pot will never see water boil," said Papa in a silly voice.

"He did not!" argued Mimi with a giggle.

"Who is Confusion?" asked Grant.

"*Confucius,*" corrected Papa. "He was a famous Chinese philosopher who had helpful reminders in the form of special sayings."

"Papa?" said Grant.

"Yes," said Papa.

"That sounds just like you!" Grant said with a loud sigh. "You always have special reminders that you say loud and clear to kids."

Papa howled with laughter, attracting attention from the surrounding crowd.

Mimi gave Papa the Evil Eye, as Grant and Christina called it. "And Mimi always has Special Reminders for me, doesn't she?" Papa teased in a quieter voice and his grandchildren laughed.

Suddenly, they found that they had passed all the international traveler hurdles and were free to leave the airport. As they waited for a taxi, Christina asked, "Just how big is the country of China?"

Papa pretended to count on an "air" abacus, his fingers flying. "Let's see: China is so big it covers 50 degrees of latitude. It includes almost four million square miles. It is bordered by 14 different countries. It has a coastline more than 12,000 miles long. And, 20 percent of the people in the world live here."

"Wow!" said Grant. "How did you know all that?"

Papa nodded at a poster on a nearby wall. "I read it right there!"

"And Beijing is the capital," said Christina. "Where our pen pals live. I love getting postcards from them with neat stamps."

"Yes," said Papa. "Your pen pals and more than a billion of their friends live in China!"

Grant and Christina were quiet with awe at the massive numbers their grandfather tossed around, as a taxi van pulled up. However, when the taxi doors slid open, both kids began to squeal.

"Li!" screamed Christina.

"Cong!" shouted Grant.

Write your own Mystery!

M ake up a dramatic title!

Y ou can pick four real kid characters!

S elect a real place for the story's setting!

T ry writing your first draft!

E dit your first draft!

R ead your final draft aloud!

Y ou can add art, photos or illustrations!

Share your book with others and
send me a copy!

Would you ~~CAROLE MARSH MYSTERIES~~ like to be
a character in a Carole Marsh Mystery?

If you would like to star in a Carole Marsh Mystery, fill
out the form below and write a 25-word paragraph
about why you think you would make a good character!
Once you're done, ask your mom or dad to send this
page to:

> Carole Marsh Mysteries Fan Club
> Gallopade International
> P.O. Box 2779
> Peachtree City, GA 30269

My name is: _____

I am a:____boy ___ girl Age:_____

I live at: _____

City:_____ State:____ Zip code:_____

My e-mail address: _____

My phone number is: _____

_____

_____

_____

_____

_____

_____

_____

_____

Visit the <u>carolemarshmysteries.com</u> website to:

- Join the Carole Marsh Mysteries™ Fan Club!

- Write a letter to Christina, Grant, Mimi, or Papa!

- Cast your vote for where the next mystery should take place!

- Find fascinating facts about the countries where the mysteries take place!

- Track your reading on an international map!

- Take the Fact or Fiction online quiz!

- Play the Around-the-World Scavenger Hunt computer game!

- Find out where the *Mystery Girl* is flying next!